LORENZO AND ANGELINA

EUGENE FERN

To my wife, Claire

Library of Congress catalog card number 68-29466
Published simultaneously in Canada
Printed in the United States of America

First printing, 1968

EUGENE FERN

Lorenzo and Angelina

Farrar, Straus & Giroux / New York

An Ariel Book

ANGELINA'S STORY

My name is Angelina García. I am nine years old. In my family are Mama, Papa, seven brothers, and six sisters. We live on a small farm high up in the Mountains of God, from which, it is said, you can see the whole universe.

We are not rich but neither do we starve, for we own a small flock of sheep, some goats, a few chickens, and a donkey. Everyone helps out in our family. My favorite job is to bring the goats' milk and the eggs to the village, even though I have so much trouble with Lorenzo.

LORENZO'S STORY

My name is Lorenzo. I am not old, not young, but somewhere in the middle. I am of the García family. They are a good family. I have always lived with them. But in all those years I have never understood them . . .

. . . least of all, Angelina!

ANGELINA'S STORY

Every morning, when the air is fresh and the dew lies like shining jewels over the fields and trees, I go to Lorenzo's stable. I carry with me the milk which Umberto has put into a heavy wooden barrel and the eggs which Jacinta has carefully packed in a wooden box. I open the door and out comes Lorenzo. "Good morning, my Lorenzo," I say. I pat his back, rub the top of his head, and give him a hug. Then I pack the barrel and box on him and I am ready to leave for the village.

But not Lorenzo!

LORENZO'S STORY

Every morning, when Angelina comes to let me out of my house, she is glad to see me. She rubs my head, puts her face next to mine, gives me a squeeze, and says, "Good morning, my Lorenzo."

And every morning, to be sure, I am glad to see her too—that is, until she starts to scold.

ANGELINA'S STORY

Every morning it is the same. I talk to him politely, but he looks this way and that. He smells the air. He chews the grass. He nibbles at the clover. He does everything but what he is supposed to do!

I begin to lose my temper, of course. I shout at him. He pays no attention. I scream! He stands like a rock. It is only when I pick up a stick that he finally moves.

Though I love him dearly, there is no doubt that my Lorenzo is the most stubborn creature in the whole world.

LORENZO'S STORY

Every morning Angelina says, "Lorenzo, it is time for us to go to the village, so please begin to walk." But anyone should know I am not yet ready to go. I have to smell the morning air. I have to chew the grass under the eucalyptus tree.

"Lorenzo," she says, "let us go this very minute." But I am still too busy. "Move, you stubborn donkey!" she screams. "Move, you block of wood! Move those stubborn feet!"

But of course I have to see if the house is in the right place, if the south fence has moved, if the sheep are where they're supposed to be. Naturally, I cannot leave yet.

It is only when she stamps her feet that I move. I am very fond of Angelina and don't like to see her upset, but is it not wrong for her to insult me this way?

One morning, like all the other times, we finally set out for the village. My stubborn Lorenzo had finished whatever it was he was doing, and I could tell by the way his ears stood straight up and by the quick movements of his feet that he was as pleased as I to leave for the marketplace at Cuzoroca.

One morning we finally set out for the village. Angelina had finished shouting and stamping. As always, she was happy once we started. I could tell by the way she began to sing and laugh—and every once in a while to skip along the road. She liked the little trip to the village and, to tell the truth, so did I.

However, this day was to be different, for I had decided to go to the top of El Padre Mountain! Ever since I can remember, I had heard of the beauty and the glory to be seen from there. It is said that from the top of El Padre one can see God's smile, feel His touch, and hear His sigh.

I was so excited about my great adventure that I hardly knew where I was going.

This day was like all other days. We went beside El Padre Mountain, through Quesada Pass, across the flat meadows, through the forest, and into the village.

ANGELINA'S STORY

When we came to the marketplace I quickly took care of my business with Señor Vives. He counted the eggs, weighed the milk, and paid me for them. I thanked him politely and played with Popo, his cute little dog, for a few moments. Then I climbed on Lorenzo's back. I could hardly wait to begin the trip to the top of El Padre Mountain!

As one might expect, when we came to the crossroads my stubborn donkey refused to move. Only after much kicking and shouting did he agree to take the right fork instead of the left.

Señor Vives was at his place, as usual. He took the milk and eggs from my back, counted the eggs, weighed the milk, and paid Angelina for them. As usual, he took the money from his strong little box under the counter. Also as usual, his pest of a dog tried to nip at my heels, but a few kicks were enough to make him stop. Then, as usual, we started for home.

But things no longer went as usual, for Angelina decided to go home a different way. Instead of taking the left turn after the road leaves the forest, she decided to take the right. At first I wouldn't budge. Who knows what might be in a strange land? Finally, with all her shouting and kicking, I gave in and went where *she* wanted to go!

This road was different from the hard dirt road leading to our farm. It passed over rushing streams, between tall trees and huge rocks, always moving up —higher and higher. It was rough and rocky, and the higher we went, the rougher it got. Though I knew the sun would soon be sinking, I was determined to reach the top of El Padre Mountain. Lorenzo moved more and more slowly, but I urged him on.

Soon the road had almost disappeared. There was nothing ahead of us but a little rocky path. It was getting dark and Lorenzo stopped. Again I had to shout and scold until he moved on.

This road was not like the other. It was rough and rocky. It did not go through Quesada Pass but behind it, toward the top of El Padre Mountain. Higher and higher we climbed, and the higher we went, the harder it was to see the road. Soon there was no road at all, just a rocky path.

And still Angelina had to explore!

Once or twice I stopped, but she shouted so much that I kept moving. It was growing dark and we were up so high I could hardly breathe. There were rocks on all sides and every once in a while a poor little bush.

Though the wind was stronger and the path even rockier than before, I was not worried. My Lorenzo is as sure-footed as a mountain goat and I knew he would not fall. Besides, any moment I expected to see the glory and beauty of our country, and this would make everything worthwhile.

But once more my stubborn donkey refused to go. Again I had to scream to make him move those stubborn legs.

LORENZO'S STORY

I was getting worried. It was not easy to walk, and I knew that if I stumbled we would have a long fall before we reached the good earth again.

So once more I stopped, but my little Angelina insisted on climbing that mountain! She shouted. She kicked. She pulled my ears. "Stubborn, stubborn donkey!" she screamed at me.

So what was there to do but move higher and still higher?

It was when we came to two huge rocks that stood like sentinels over the others that Lorenzo made up his mind not to move another inch. He sat down in front of the rocks in such a way that not even a tiny lizard could pass by.

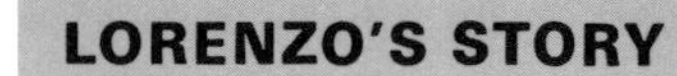

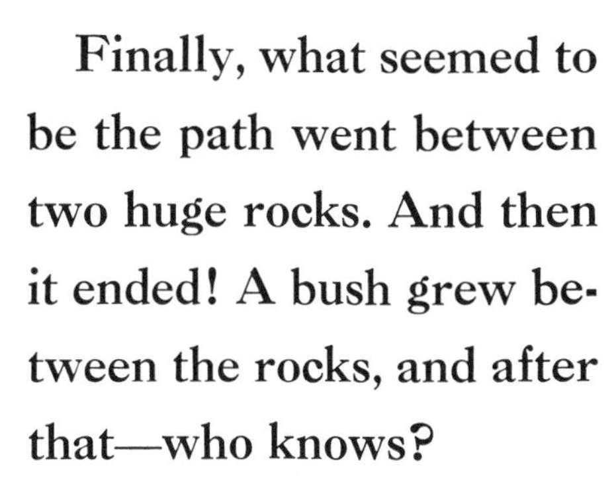

Finally, what seemed to be the path went between two huge rocks. And then it ended! A bush grew between the rocks, and after that—who knows?

This time I decided the trip was over. Not another step would I take!

I sat down.

I yelled at Lorenzo. I shouted. I pleaded. I screamed. I pulled at him. I pushed him from behind. He would not budge. He sat there looking like one more rock among all the others.

The great explorer Angelina did not take to this kindly. Her shouts before were as nothing compared to the noise she now made. "Move!" she screamed. "We are almost at the top. Move, you stubborn son of a stubborn two-headed goat!" She kicked and pushed and pulled me. Tears of anger were in her eyes, but it did no good. This time I would not take another step.

At this very moment I heard footsteps, and there behind us appeared my father, followed by Señor Vives and Señor Quiñones of the police. Suddenly I realized how late it must be. I was sure Papa would be furious. Instead he picked me up and kissed me. All he said was:

"Little one, I am not angry because you took the right turn instead of the left. Children are always looking for new paths. This I understand. But why have you stayed so long? Didn't you know your mother and I would be worried? Everyone is looking for you."

I tried to explain how much I wanted to see the glory of the world from the top of El Padre Mountain and how much time I had wasted trying to get that stubborn Lorenzo to move.

Suddenly there were sounds behind us and who should appear but Señor García, Señor Vives, and Señor Quiñones of the police! How happy they were to see us! Señor García picked up little Angelina. He hugged her and whispered to her, while the other gentlemen, with big smiles, slapped him on the back.

Angelina looked ashamed and said, "I did so much want to see the top of the mountain, Papa, but that stubborn Lorenzo would not move. He simply refused to budge."

Papa said nothing. He took my hand and led me between the two huge rocks. He pushed the little bush aside so I could see beyond it. I looked and my knees turned to water! Beyond the bush was the end of the path and also the end of the mountain. Had Lorenzo and I taken but one step beyond the bush, we should never have taken a step again!

Señor García did not say a word. He took Angelina by the hand and led her between the two rocks. Beyond the bush was nothing—no path, no rocks, just nothing.

It was, of course, as *I* suspected. What could one expect to find up here so near the sky, where even the poorest bush finds it difficult to breathe?

Angelina said nothing. She just stood there, pale and trembling. My poor Angelina!

I do not remember too clearly what happened after that, for I was weak from fear and could hardly stand. But I do remember one thing. Seeing that dear, stubborn donkey standing there, I felt such a love for him that I kissed him gently and whispered, "Thank you, my Lorenzo!"

Señor García said, "You should be grateful to have such a stubborn donkey, my little flower. If not for him, I would have neither Angelina nor Lorenzo." He put his arms around my neck and gave me such a squeeze that I could hardly breathe. When Angelina kissed me, my happiness was complete.

ANGELINA'S STORY

Things have not changed much on our farm since our little adventure. Of course I sometimes go back with Lorenzo to the top of El Padre, stand by the little bush, and look down at the glorious world. The entire province stretches like a rich carpet before one's eyes, while the Mountains of God stand watching over all. It is beautiful indeed.

As for Lorenzo, I do not scold him so much, and in the mornings I let him do whatever it is he seems to like to do for as long as he likes to do it. After all, though I am even more certain now that there was never a more stubborn creature than Lorenzo, his very stubbornness saved our lives.

Could it be that stubborn donkeys were made just for girls like me?

LORENZO'S STORY

Everything has changed on our farm since Angelina's adventure. Every morning when we leave for the market she lets me chew the grass, smell the morning air, and look around to see that everything is where it is supposed to be—for as long as I like to do so. And when *I* am ready to go, then we leave. She does not shout at me or stamp her feet. And no longer does she call me stubborn.

This is how it should be, of course, for she loves me as I love her.

And, after all, who was stubborn—she or I?